W9-BRT-073

The Little Red Stroller

Joshua Furst  illustrated by **Katy Wu**

Dial Books for  Young Readers

Dial Books for Young Readers
Penguin Young Readers Group
An imprint of Penguin Random House LLC
375 Hudson Street
New York, NY 10014

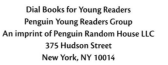

Text copyright © 2019 by Joshua Furst
Illustrations copyright © 2019 by Katy Wu

Published by Penguin

Penguin supports copyright. Copyright fuels creativity, encourages diverse voices,
promotes free speech, and creates a vibrant culture.
Thank you for buying an authorized edition of this book and for complying with
copyright laws by not reproducing, scanning, or distributing any part of it in
any form without permission. You are supporting writers and allowing
Penguin to continue to publish books for every reader.

Library of Congress Cataloging-in-Publication Data

Names: Furst, Joshua, date, author. | Wu, Katy, illustrator.
Title: The little red stroller / Joshua Furst ; illustrated by Katy Wu.
Description: New York, NY : Dial Books for Young Readers, [2019]
Summary: Luna outgrows her stroller just as Ernie needs one,
and when he outgrows it he passes it along to Gigi, and soon many
different families have received and shared the gift.
Identifiers: LCCN 2017057434 | ISBN 9780735228801 (hardcover)
Subjects: | CYAC: Baby strollers—Fiction. | Families—Fiction. | Generosity—Fiction.
Classification: LCC PZ7.1.F985 Lit 2019 | DDC [E]—dc23
LC record available at https://lccn.loc.gov/2017057434

Printed in China
1 3 5 7 9 10 8 6 4 2

Design by Jasmin Rubero
Text set in Cronos Pro Semibold

The art for this book was created digitally.

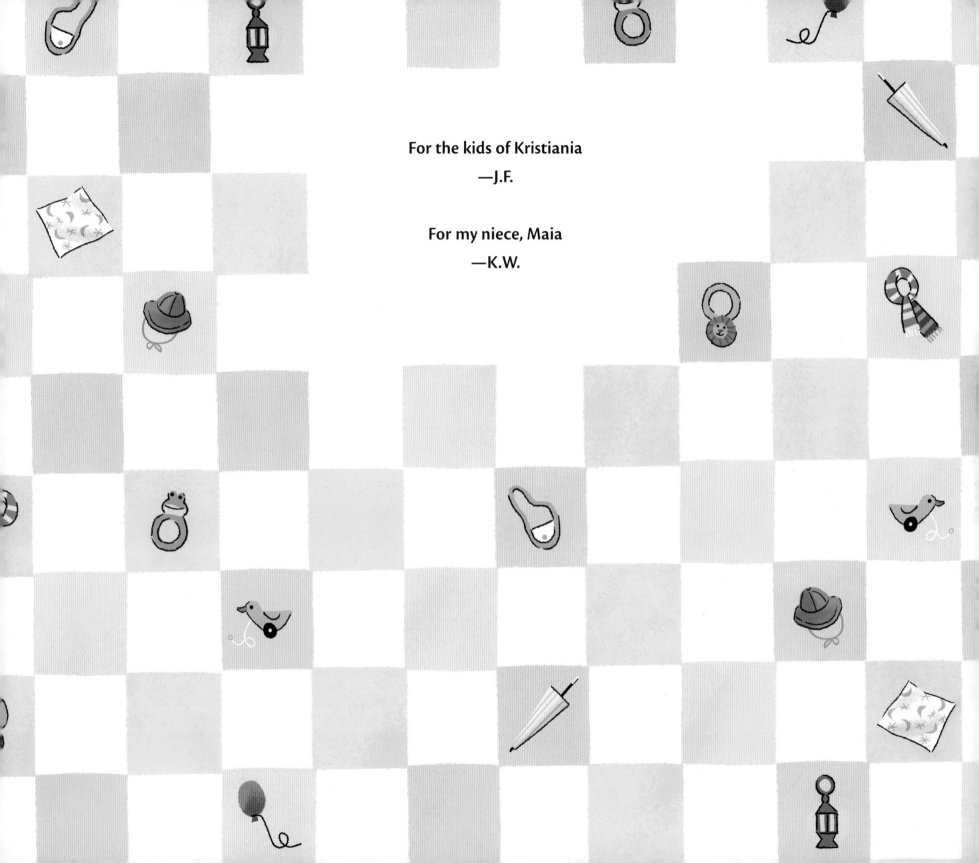

For the kids of Kristiania

—J.F.

For my niece, Maia

—K.W.

A long time ago, when Luna was just two weeks old,
her mommy gave her a little red stroller.

For now, it lived in the hallway.

But as Luna got bigger, she used it to go to school and the playground.

And on weekends, Luna and her mommy and the little red stroller wandered up and down the avenue, from the bagel place to the flower shop to the pizzeria where Luna liked to get her favorite, olive pizza.

One day, Luna bumped into her downstairs neighbor Ernie and his mommy and daddy.

"We wish we had a little red stroller like yours," they told Luna.

"I'm too big for my stroller now. Why don't you take it?" Luna said.

So they did.

And on sunny days, Ernie and his mommy and daddy and the little red stroller roamed around the park,

from the Japanese garden

to the mini-train
that went through tunnels

to the carousel where
Ernie got to ride the lion.

One day, Ernie and his mommy and daddy had lunch with Gigi.
Gigi and her daddy were going on a trip to visit Gigi's grandpa.

"We wish we had a stroller to take with us," Gigi's daddy said.

"We got this little red stroller from Luna, but I'm too big for it now.
Why don't you take it?" said Ernie.

So they did.

And Gigi and her daddy and the little red stroller
meandered all over the cute little town where Gigi's grandpa lived,
from the river to the farmer's market

to her grandpa's house, where he cooked a yummy meal
in a special pot called a pressure cooker.

One day, long after they got home, Gigi and her daddy met Callie at the playground.

Callie and her two mommies were going to a birthday party.

"We wish we had a stroller like yours," one of Callie's mommies said.

"We got this little red stroller from Ernie, but I'm too big for it now," said Gigi.

"Why don't you take it?"

So they did.

And Callie and her mommies and the little red stroller
rolled all the way to the birthday party,
where they saw a magic show and ate ice cream cake
and dressed up as pirates to go on a treasure hunt.

Callie found a doubloon!

One day, after she'd been to many more birthday parties,
Callie and her mommies had dinner with Taj.
Taj and his mommy and daddy were going to the countryside to visit a farm.

"We wish we had a stroller to take with us," Taj's mommy and daddy said.

"We got this little red stroller from Gigi," Callie said.

"But I'm too big for it now. Why don't you take it?"

So they did.

And Taj and his mommy and daddy and the little red stroller rambled all around the farm, from the field where they chased chickens to the barn where they fed alpacas

to the stand where Taj got to drink some
really yummy apple cider.

APPLE CIDER
FOR
SALE

One day, Taj and his mommy
and daddy met Kavi.
Kavi and his mommy and daddy
were going to the beach.

Like Callie and Gigi and Ernie and Taj,
and even Luna, who was getting to be a pretty big girl now,
Kavi needed a stroller.

And like Callie

and Gigi

and Ernie

and Luna,

and their mommies and daddies,
and mommies and mommies, and
daddy, and mommy,

Taj and his mommy and daddy gave
the little red stroller to Kavi . . .

who clacked along the boardwalk with it before . . .

giving it to Sula and her two daddies,
who marched in a Halloween parade with it, and then . . .

gave it to Caroline and her mommy and daddy,

who took it camping in the mountains before . . .

they gave it to Maxine and her mommy and daddy,

who went all the way to Texas and back with it before . . .

they gave it to Selah and his mommy and daddy.

SCHOOL

LITTLE DINER

BAGEL HUT

FLOWERS

BOUQUETS

PIZZA

After traveling up and down the avenue and around the park and all over the cute little town by the river,

and to about a hundred birthday parties,

CANDY

WATERMELON

FLOWERS

JUICE

WELCOME

BAKERY

FRESH!

to say nothing of marching
in a Halloween parade,

and to a farm
and to the beach,

and camping in the mountains
and going all the way to Texas and back,

the little red stroller was so tattered
and tired, it could go no farther.

One day when they were out with the little red stroller,

Selah and his mommy and daddy sat on the steps of a museum feeling sad.

When Ben and his mommy saw them crying, Ben asked, "What's wrong?"

"Our little red stroller has broken," said Selah's mommy and daddy.

Ben and his mommy thought about this
and then they had an idea.
"We have a little *yellow* stroller," Ben said.
"I'm too big for it now. Why don't you take it?"

So they did.

And since it was summer and there was a free music festival happening in the park, Selah and his mommy and daddy and the little yellow stroller wandered over to eat corn on the cob and cheesy arepas and sing along to songs they knew by heart.

One day, Selah and his mommy and daddy met Luna, who'd grown up by then and had a baby of her own. His name was Isaiah and he was just two weeks old.

When Selah saw that Isaiah didn't have a stroller, he said, "We got this little yellow stroller from Ben, but I'm too big for it now. Why don't you take it?"

And so Luna's baby, Isaiah, did.